The GUMBY™ Book of Shapes

Jane Hyman

DOUBLEDAY & COMPANY, INC.
GARDEN CITY, NEW YORK

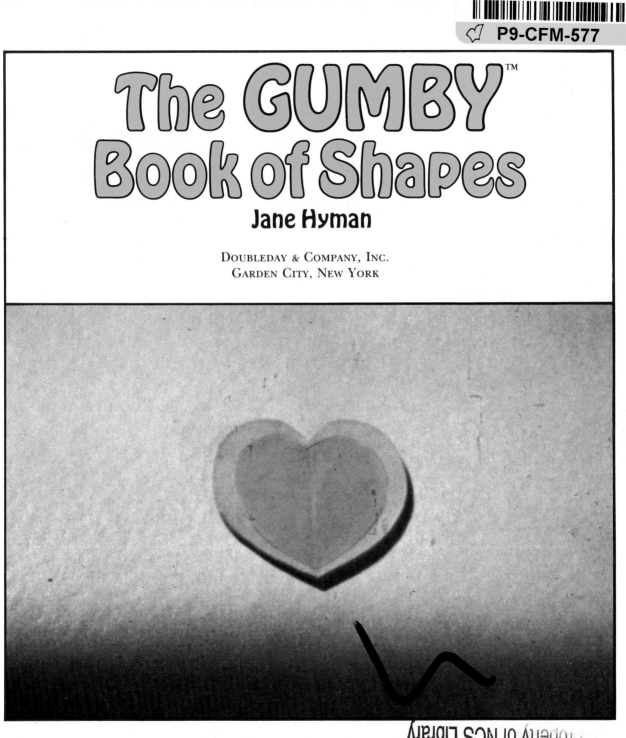

For Muriel Watson, Theresa Gregoire, and
Connie Redmond, three wonderful women
who have helped me enormously . . .
                                    Thank you!!

Library of Congress Cataloging-in-Publication Data

Hyman, Jane.
    The Gumby book of shapes.

    Summary: Clay figures Gumby and Pokey introduce basic
shapes, including the circle, square, rectangle, triangle, oval,
and heart.
    1. Geometry—Juvenile literature.   [1. Shape]
I. Title.
QA447.H96 1986   516   86–6194
ISBN 0-385-23453-8 Trade.
ISBN 0-385-23848-7 Lib. bdg.
Copyright © 1986 by Art Clokey.

Licensed through Lorimar Licensing Corporation

For Grown-Ups

Do you remember Gumby? He's that little green blob of clay who brings fun and enjoyment to children of all ages. Let Gumby help you spend some quality time with your child as you both discover that learning with Gumby and his friends can be creative and rewarding.

Pick a special place that's comfortable and peaceful. Keep all distractions to a minimum. Perhaps you'll want to set aside a specific time each day for you and your youngster to read the book together. Make this a private time between you and your child. You both deserve to learn from each other.

This book has been designed to expose your child to the basic shapes. These shapes include circle, square, rectangle, triangle, oval, and heart. Most of the emphasis has been placed on distinguishing the basic characteristics of a circle, a square, and a rectangle. Your child will have many opportunities to find these shapes in a variety of photographs throughout the book. Because Gumby and his friends are made of clay, and molding clay can be both fun and educational, it is suggested that you might want to use some clay with your child and build these shapes together.

After you have read the story, you might want to look around your house to find objects that are examples of the basic shapes. Some objects might be made of combinations of shapes. For example, the front door may be a large rectangle and the door knob may be round.

Have a wonderful time together. Remember, you are your child's first teacher and your home is your youngster's first school. Enjoy!

 He was once a little green blob of clay. At first the clay was shaped like a **round** ball.

Then the clay was flattened
into a **rectangle**.

 And Gumby was made out of that green rectangle.

His friend Pokey was once an orange slab of clay. Do you see the orange **rectangle**?

 Pokey was made out of that
rectangle. Gumby's
rectangle is tall and thin.
Pokey's rectangle is
short and fat.

Do you see the orange and green squares? All the squares are the same size. All sides of each square are the same size, too.

Hi, boys and girls. My name
is Gumby.

Follow me inside this book.
Pokey and I are hunting for
shapes.

 There are our old enemies the blockheads. Look at their heads. Each head is shaped like a square.

I remember when the blockheads tried to change the shape of Prickle's head and Pokey's head. My friends had square heads.

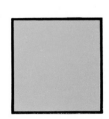

 The blockheads used a special shape machine. Do you see the needle pointing to the square?

I had to come to the rescue.
I made the needle point to
the circle. Can you see the
circle?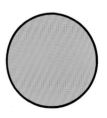

 First I made square heads into round heads. Poor blockheads.

No more **square** heads for Prickle and Pokey!

Oh how I love a good race. I
remember when Pokey and I
were in the Racing Game.

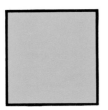 The racing board had
squares and **circles**.
Can you see them?
It had X's, too.

 Here's a good look at the racing board. How many **circles** and **squares** can you find?

Even the time clock in the race looks like a giant circle. That's because it is round.

 Look at me now! There are two of me! I'm making music by playing two **round** cymbals.

Now I'm playing a triangle.
It's a musical instrument in
the shape of a triangle.

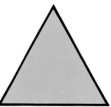

My two friends Too and Loo are **oval**-shaped musical notes. They love to hear me play.

There are a lot of **ovals** in this picture. Each watermelon is shaped like an **oval**.

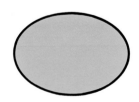 And the giant egg that landed on my father's car is an **oval**, too!

Thanks for joining us. Pokey and I sure had fun finding all the circles, squares, rectangles, ovals, and triangles.
Did you see them all?

Remember, if you have a **heart**, then Gumby's a part of you.